✔ KT-549-768

Lottie
the Lollipop
Fairy

by Daisy Meadows

ORCHARD

www.rainbowmagic.co.uk

The Fairyland Palace

Candy Land

Goblins' ice cream van

Market St

Charlie's ice cream

Kirsty's Hou

Wetherbury Village

Jack Frost's
Ice Castle

Funfair

The Park

Sweet
Shop

The High St.

Jack Frost's Spell

I have a plan to cause some strife
And use those fairies to change my life.
I'm going to take their charms away
And make my dreams come true today!

I'll build a castle made of sweets,
And spoil the fairies' silly treats.
I just don't care how much they whine,
Their cakes and lollies will be mine!

Contents

Not So Sweet!

"I can't *wait* for you to meet my aunt, Rachel!" Kirsty Tate exclaimed, beaming at her best friend, Rachel Walker. Rachel had arrived that morning to spend the spring half-term holiday with Kirsty in the pretty village of Wetherbury. "Mum's invited her to come to lunch today, so you'll be able to ask Aunt Harri all about *Candy Land*."

Rachel grinned. "I can't wait to meet Aunt Harri, either," she replied. "Working in a sweet factory must be one of the most wonderful jobs in the whole world!"

"I guess it's *almost* as wonderful as being a fairy," Kirsty said, and the girls shared a secret smile. They'd had many thrilling adventures with their fairy friends and hoped to have lots more.

"The *Candy Land* factory is on a hill overlooking Wetherbury," Kirsty explained. "Aunt Harri gets lots of free sweets and she always brings a big bagful of treats with her whenever she comes to visit."

"Oh, I'm looking forward to meeting her even more, then!" Rachel laughed.

There was a ring at the doorbell and the girls rushed to answer it. Outside stood a smiling, fair-haired young woman holding a bulging pink-and-white striped carrier bag. *Candy Land* was written across the side of the bag in sparkly silver glitter.

"Hello, Kirsty," Aunt Harri said, giving her a big hug. "And you must be Rachel." She hugged Rachel, too. "I've heard so much about you from Kirsty."

"I've heard lots about you, too," Rachel replied, smiling back.

"Then I'm sure Kirsty's told you all about *Candy Land*!" Aunt Harri said, her big blue eyes twinkling. "I thought you might like to try some of our

sweets." And she handed the bag to the girls.

Eagerly, Rachel and Kirsty peeked inside.

They could see lollipops, chocolate bars, and piles of other sweets wrapped in shiny coloured paper. However, to their dismay, the sweets looked broken and battered and not at all appetising. But, most unexpected of all, there was a

horrible smell inside
the bag that
made both
girls gasp and
draw back
slightly. What
on earth
was that
smell, Rachel
thought,
trying not to
wrinkle up her

nose in disgust. The
sweets looked and smelt like rotting
rubbish! But she didn't want to be rude
and complain when Aunt Harri had
been kind enough to bring them the
sweets. Kirsty, too, was trying to smile
politely at her aunt.

"Maybe we should wait until after lunch to try them," Kirsty suggested, closing the bag quickly.

Aunt Harri's face fell. "The sweets are really bad, aren't they?" she sighed. "Girls, something's gone terribly wrong at *Candy Land*. All the sweets look, smell and taste absolutely horrid!"

Rachel and Kirsty were too shocked to speak.

"We've had lots of complaints," Aunt Harri went on, looking more and more upset. "Tracy Twist from the village sweet shop even phoned the factory to tell us her customers were *very* unhappy about it."

"Has the factory changed the sweet

14

recipes?" Rachel asked curiously.

Aunt Harri shook her head. "Our sweets have been made the same way for years," she replied. "All the ingredients are still the same. That's why it's so strange!"

"That *is* odd," Kirsty remarked, frowning. The sweets from *Candy Land* were usually delicious. What on earth was going on, she wondered.

Mrs Tate had prepared a delicious lunch, and, as they ate, Rachel and Kirsty were glad to see that Aunt Harri soon began to cheer up. After lunch Aunt Harri said goodbye and then hurried back to work at the sweet factory. Meanwhile the girls went up to Kirsty's bedroom, taking the *Candy Land* bag with them.

"Let's sort through the sweets," Kirsty said. "Maybe some of them aren't so bad." So she and Rachel sat down on the rug and tipped out the contents of the bag.

Wrinkling her nose because of the dreadful smell, Rachel selected a chocolate bar. She unwrapped the gold foil and took a cautious bite.

"That's horrible!" Rachel spluttered, pulling a face. "It tastes like washing-up liquid, really nasty and soapy."

Kirsty chose a lollipop covered in shiny gold cellophane. The lollipop was bent out of shape and cracked across the middle, and the cellophane was torn in places. The tatty label stuck on the front said *Strawberry Flavour*.

"Here goes!" Kirsty murmured, pulling off the cellophane. She licked the lollipop, then groaned. "It smells of old socks – and it tastes like them, too!"

"Let's not try anything else," Rachel said. "The others could be even worse!"

Disappointed, the girls began scooping the sweets back into the bag. The gold wrapper from the soapy chocolate bar was lying on the rug, and as Rachel went to pick it up, she *thought* she saw the wrapper move.

Rachel blinked and looked again. Yes, the chocolate bar wrapper was definitely moving all on its own! Carefully Rachel lifted the wrapper up and underneath she saw a familiar little figure waving up at her.

"Look, Kirsty, it's Honey the Sweet Fairy!" Rachel exclaimed, delighted to see their old friend.

Kirsty's eyes widened in surprise. "It's great to see you, Honey!" she said. The girls had had some wonderful adventures with Honey and the other Party Fairies when they'd helped them retrieve their magical party objects from Jack Frost's goblins.

"Hello, girls." Honey fluttered up to perch on the edge of Kirsty's bed. "I expect you can guess why I'm here, can't you?"

19

"Because of the horrible sweets from *Candy Land*?" asked Rachel.

Honey nodded. "Strange things are happening in Fairyland!" she sighed. "We're in trouble again, girls, and we need your help. Will you come?"

"Of course!" Kirsty said immediately, and Rachel nodded.

"You're our very best friends in the whole of the fairy and the human worlds!" Honey said gratefully. "Let's go right away, and I'll explain everything as soon as we get there."

And with one flick of Honey's wand, a shower of fairy sparkles swept the three of them off to Fairyland.

Candy Castle

A few moments later Rachel, Kirsty and Honey floated down into the Fairyland Sweet Factory. This was a beautiful, magical orchard where all the sweets grew on trees. The girls had been to the orchard before and had been amazed by all the gorgeous candy hanging in huge clusters among the pale-green sugared leaves. But this time it looked very different.

"What's happened?" Rachel asked, staring around the orchard in dismay. The girls could see that the candy trees looked tired and wilted, the sugared leaves withering away on the branches. The sweets growing on the trees also looked pale and sickly instead of fresh and luscious. Kirsty reached up and touched a pink-and-white marshmallow dangling from a branch over her head.

"The marshmallows are rock-hard!" Kirsty said, shocked.

"And the gobstoppers are as soft as butter," added Rachel, who was standing beneath a gobstopper tree. She also noticed that all the chocolates on the tree next to her were melting into a gooey mess and dripping from the branches, leaving puddles on the ground. Even the sherbet fountain was spouting thick grey sludge instead of sparkling golden sherbet. This was just like what was happening at *Candy Land*, Rachel thought.

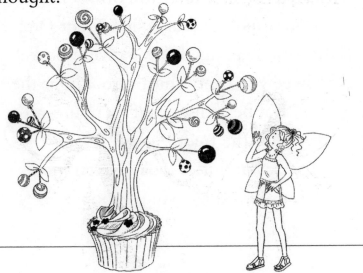

King Oberon and Queen Titania were standing beside the sherbet fountain, deep in discussion with seven other fairies. They all looked extremely worried. Then the queen noticed Honey, Kirsty and Rachel hurrying towards them.

"Girls, you've come!' Queen Titania gasped with relief. "We really do need your help. Our beautiful Sweet Factory is ruined!"

"And the day after tomorrow is a special royal festival called Treat Day," the king explained. "We give a basket of sweets to every fairy throughout the land. It'll be a disaster if there are no sweets for the treat baskets!"

The seven fairies looked even more anxious and their wings drooped miserably. Honey turned to Rachel and Kirsty. "Girls, meet my special helpers, the Sweet Fairies," she announced, pointing at each fairy in turn with her wand. "Lottie the Lollipop Fairy, Esme the Ice Cream Fairy, Coco the Cupcake Fairy, Clara the Chocolate Fairy, Madeleine the Cookie Fairy, Layla the Candyfloss Fairy and Nina the Birthday Cake Fairy."

"Welcome, girls," the fairies chorused.

"We hope you can help us," Lottie the Lollipop Fairy added. She was a particularly pretty little fairy with curly blonde hair, and she wore a silky green dress with colourful pink, yellow and purple stripes, tied at the front with a big purple bow.

"Is Jack Frost up to his naughty tricks again?" asked Kirsty, and all the fairies nodded sadly.

"He's stolen our seven magical objects!" Lottie explained. "He wants all our delicious sweets for a very special project."

"What special project?" Rachel asked curiously.

Honey led the girls over to one of the
pools of melted chocolate
on the ground. She
waved her wand and
gradually the brown
puddle became clear.
Then a picture
began to appear.
Rachel and Kirsty
could see the
Fairyland stream
surrounded by lush green hills.

"Look!" Honey pointed at one of the
hills. "See that castle?"

Rachel and Kirsty peered more closely
at the picture. On top of the hill a huge
castle was taking shape. It was only half
built, but there was something else very
peculiar about it.

"The castle's made of *sweets*!" Kirsty exclaimed suddenly. "Rachel, see the cupcake turrets and the doors made of cookies?"

Rachel nodded. "And the towers are ice cream cones!" she added.

The girls could see Jack Frost's goblins dashing around the castle with wheelbarrows of cupcakes, ice cream cones, chocolate bars, candyfloss and other sweets. Jack Frost himself was standing on the scaffolding, yelling at them.

"Hurry, you lazy good-for-nothings!" he shouted. "I want my sweetie castle finished as quickly as possible. I've been planning it for *ages* because sweets are one of my most favourite things. And bring me a lemon cupcake – I'm hungry!"

"See that necklace around Jack Frost's neck?" Honey pointed her wand at the picture in the chocolate pool. Rachel and Kirsty stared at the necklace. It had seven glittering candy charms on it. "Those are the Sweet Fairies' magical objects!"

One of the goblins rushed over and handed Jack Frost a cupcake. "I bet those pesky fairies will try to get their magical charms back before Treat Day," the goblin pointed out.

Jack Frost gave a roar of rage. "Treat Day is cancelled!" he snapped. "And I'll make *sure* those silly fairies and their human friends don't try to interfere!" Jack Frost waved his wand, and a bolt of icy magic surrounded him.

When the frosty air melted away, Rachel and Kirsty saw that the Sweet Fairies' magical objects had disappeared from the necklace Jack Frost was wearing.

"Now those charms are safe in the hands of my goblins!" Jack Frost cackled smugly. "They've hidden them away in the human world, so the Sweet Fairies will never see their charms again! Ha ha!"

Tracy Twist's Sweet Shop

King Oberon sighed as the picture in the pool of chocolate faded. "So you see, girls, Treat Day will be ruined unless our Sweet Fairies get their magical objects back," he explained. "Without them, our Fairyland Sweet Factory will simply wither away and die."

"And all sweets in the human world will be spoilt, too," Lottie the Lollipop Fairy chimed in. "Just like the ones from *Candy Land*."

"Girls, will you help the Sweet Fairies to save Treat Day?" Queen Titania asked hopefully.

The girls nodded. "We'll do our best," replied Kirsty in a determined voice, and all the fairies clapped happily.

"Lottie will return with you to Wetherbury," Honey said, pointing her wand at Rachel and Kirsty. "Thank you, girls!"
Then a stream of
magical fairy
dust whisked
Lottie and the
girls away,
the good–
luck wishes of
the other fairies
ringing in their ears.

"Where should we start searching for the magical objects?" Rachel wanted to know as soon as they were back in Kirsty's bedroom.

Lottie thought for a moment. "What about the village sweet shop?" she suggested. "The goblins might try to hide my charm among all the real lollipops there."

"Good idea!" Kirsty agreed. Lottie zipped over to hide in the pocket of Rachel's skirt and then they hurried downstairs. Quickly Kirsty asked her mum for permission to go to the sweet shop and when Mrs Tate said yes, the three friends set off right away.

"We *must* find
all seven magical
objects," Rachel
said with a
frown as she and
Kirsty walked
down the high
street. "Imagine a
world where all sweets
tasted horrible! It would be *awful*."

Kirsty nudged her. "Look, Rachel," she
murmured. "See those children coming
towards us? They're carrying bags from
the sweet shop."

The girls watched as the children came
closer. Two of them were unwrapping
chocolate bars, while the youngest of
the three, a little girl, was holding an ice
cream cone.

"Ugh! That tastes soapy!" one of them complained after taking a big bite of chocolate.

"So does mine," the other agreed. "It's the worst chocolate I've ever had in my whole life!"

The little girl took one lick of her ice cream and promptly burst into tears. "It tastes nasty!" she wailed.

"Oh dear!" Lottie murmured anxiously from inside Rachel's pocket.

"This must be happening *everywhere*," Kirsty pointed out. "The sooner we get all the magical objects back to the Sweet Fairies, the sooner the sweets will taste good again!"

Kirsty opened the door of the village sweet shop and she and Rachel went inside. The shop was empty and the owner, Tracy Twist, was sitting at the counter, looking very glum. The shop was packed with all kinds of sweets in big glass jars. Boxes of chocolates, cupcakes and cookies were stacked around.

There were lots of different flavours of ice cream to choose from, as well as a candyfloss machine. But the girls couldn't spot a single lollipop.

"Hi, girls," said Tracy. She looked at Kirsty. "I expect Aunt Harri has told you all about the problems with the *Candy Land* sweets?" Kirsty nodded and Tracy heaved a big sigh. "I'm losing all my customers because the sweets taste so bad!" Tracy went on. "And no one seems to know why."

"Actually, we've come to buy some lollipops," Kirsty said, glancing around the shop. "Do you have any, Tracy?"

Tracy shook her head. "I sold *all* my lollipops this morning to a group of boys," she replied. "I don't know who they were, but they must belong to some sort of club because they were wearing matching green clothes."

Rachel and Kirsty exchanged an excited glance. Goblins?

"They started eating the lollipops before they left the shop." Tracy frowned. "And they were licking their lips and saying how wonderful they tasted! I was really surprised because I've had so many complaints about the other sweets. Maybe there were a few good ones in that batch of lollipops from *Candy Land* after all… Oh dear. My mum used to run this shop. She'd be so disappointed to know this had happened." Tracy looked around the shop, sadly.

"Those goblins have my magical charm and that's why the lollipops they bought tasted so good!" Lottie whispered to the girls. "But where are the goblins *now*?"

A Lollipop Trail

"Did the boys say where they were going, Tracy?" asked Rachel.

"No, they didn't," Tracy replied.

"Well, thanks, anyway," said Kirsty. "I'm sure that all the sweets in your shop will soon be just as delicious as they used to be."

"I hope so," Tracy sighed.

The girls hurried outside.

"We're on the goblins' trail!" Kirsty said excitedly. "But I wonder which way they went when they came out of the sweet shop?"

Both girls glanced around, but couldn't see any flashes of green that might be goblins. Then Rachel gave a cry.

"Have you spotted a goblin?" Kirsty asked eagerly.

"No, but I *have* spotted this!" Rachel replied. She bent down and picked up a wooden lollipop stick lying on the pavement. "And look, there's another one a little further ahead of us."

"The goblins are scoffing all the lollipops and leaving a trail of lollipop sticks!" Lottie exclaimed, peeking out of Rachel's pocket. "We can find them by following the trail. Girls, it'll be quicker if

I turn you into fairies. We can fly much faster than we can walk!"

There was no one around to see as Lottie whirled out of Rachel's pocket and hovered above the girls, sprinkling them with shining fairy dust. Instantly Rachel and Kirsty shrank down to the same tiny size as Lottie. Fluttering their wings, the girls rose up into the air to join their friend.

"Follow the lollipop trail!" Lottie called, and they flew off down the high street.

"The goblins must have lots of lollipops," Kirsty said with a frown, noting the lollipop sticks and wrappers lying all along the pavement. "And they're eating them super-fast! Look at all this litter."

"Don't worry, Kirsty," Lottie assured her, "I can clear up in two shakes of a fairy's wand!" And as they flew along, Lottie began waving her wand above the pavement. Clouds of fairy magic floated down, making the lollipop litter behind them vanish.

The trail turned off halfway along the high street and Lottie and the girls followed it through the winding streets of Wetherbury. Eventually they reached the local park and Rachel gave an excited shout.

"The trail ends here," she pointed out as Lottie's magic whisked away the very last lollipop stick. "The goblins must be in the park!"

Kirsty, Lottie and Rachel flew through the park gates. Ahead of them they could see four boys sitting at one of the wooden picnic tables on the grass. The boys wore matching green dungarees and baseball caps, and they were all licking giant lollipops. On the picnic table were lots of bags from the village sweet shop, all full of lollipops.

Then Rachel noticed four pairs of big
green feet sticking out from underneath
the table.

"It's the goblins!" Rachel whispered.

"Let's hide close by and listen to what
they're saying," Lottie suggested.

Lottie and the girls swooped down and
fluttered silently into a flowerbed near
the picnic table. They
tucked themselves
away among
the dazzling
golden
daffodils
and then
peeped out
to see what
the goblins
were up to.

"Mmm!" the biggest goblin sighed
happily. "These lollipops are delicious!"
He finished the one he was eating and
tossed the stick away into the flowerbed.
The stick flew towards
Rachel and she had
to duck out of the
way. Then the
goblin grabbed
another lollipop
and pulled off
the cellophane
wrapper. He
threw the wrapper

into the daffodils and it landed on top of
Lottie. Kirsty and Rachel rushed to help
her shake it off.

"You're a greedy-guts!" the smallest
goblin said accusingly to the biggest one.

"You've had lots more lovely lollipops than anyone else." He gobbled down the rest of his lollipop and immediately snatched *two* more.

"Stop that!" yelled the other two goblins. "We love the lollipops, too!" And they both scoffed the remains of their lollipops as fast as they could so that they could grab another one each.

"The goblins are enjoying the lollipops very much," Lottie murmured. "My lollipop charm is making them taste good, so that means it must be close by! But where?"

Rachel, Kirsty and Lottie stayed
hidden, hoping the goblins might
mention Lottie's lollipop charm. But they
didn't. Instead they ate their way steadily
through the huge pile of lollipops. After
a while, Rachel noticed that the goblins'
faces were looking even greener than
usual.

"I don't feel well," the smallest goblin
moaned. "I've eaten too many lollipops.
I feel sick!"

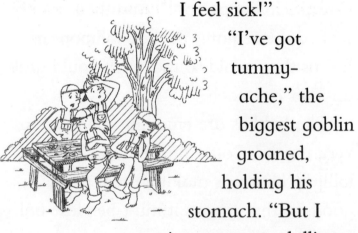

"I've got
tummy-
ache," the
biggest goblin
groaned,
holding his
stomach. "But I
want just *one* more lollipop.

And I've saved the best till last!"

The biggest goblin put his hand into the pocket at the front of his dungarees. As he pulled out a beautiful, candy-coloured lollipop, Rachel and Kirsty noticed a bracelet around the goblin's wrist. It was glimmering slightly with a magical glow.

"It's my lollipop charm!" Lottie whispered, her face alight with excitement. "Girls, we *must* get it back!"

Gobbling Goblins!

Lottie, Rachel and Kirsty burst out of the clump of daffodils and flew straight towards the picnic table.

"Hey, that's my lollipop charm bracelet!" Lottie called out.

The big goblin scowled as Lottie and the girls hovered in the air in front of him.

"Go away, you interfering fairies!"
the goblin shouted, shaking his fist.
"Jack Frost gave me
this bracelet and
told me to
look after it.
You're not
having it!"

"It's
helping us
to collect *lots*
of delicious
lollipops for
Jack Frost," the
smallest goblin said
proudly.

"We need them to make lollipop
flowers for the garden at Jack Frost's
candy castle," the big goblin added.

Kirsty pointed down at the lollipop sticks and wrappers and the empty sweet-shop bags that littered the ground around the picnic table. "And exactly how many lollipops *do* you have left for Jack Frost?" Kirsty asked.

The goblins looked down at the empty picnic table.

"You've eaten all the lollipops, haven't you?" said Kirsty.

The goblins glanced nervously at each other and Rachel could see they were beginning to panic.

"This is all your fault for being so greedy!" the biggest goblin told the smallest one. "Now we haven't got any lollipops for Jack Frost's garden."

"*You* ate more lollipops than me!" the smallest goblin screeched. "I hardly ate any of them."

"What are we going to do?" asked one
of the other two goblins. "We can't go
back to the candy castle without any
lollipops. Jack Frost will be *really* angry
with us!"

"Maybe we can help you," Rachel
said.

"How?" the goblins chorused sulkily.

"If you give Lottie her lollipop charm,
she'll be able to
magic up lots
of beautiful
lollipop
flowers for
you,"
Rachel told
them. "Won't
you, Lottie?"

Lottie nodded.

61

"Then Jack Frost will be *very* pleased with you," Rachel added, "and you won't get into trouble."

"But first you've got to clean up all this mess!" Kirsty said, pointing at the litter surrounding the picnic table. She flew down and picked up one of the lollipop wrappers.

The goblins shook their heads stubbornly.

"No way!" the biggest goblin said rudely, hiding Lottie's lollipop charm behind his back. "Go away and leave us alone!"

"Well, OK, then," said Rachel. "I just wonder what Jack Frost will do when he finds out you ate all the lollipops for his garden…"

The goblins turned a pale green.

"Wait!" the biggest goblin called as Rachel, Lottie and Kirsty pretended to fly away. "Don't go!"

"So, do you agree to give Lottie her lollipop charm back *and* clear up the litter?" Rachel asked.

Lollipop Flowers

"Yes!" the biggest goblin snapped. "Here, take it!" And he held the charm bracelet out to Lottie.

Lottie swooped down and took her bracelet from the goblin. It shimmered magically as it shrank to its Fairyland size. She put it on her wrist.

"Now you've got to keep your side of the bargain!" the big goblin demanded. "Where are our lollipop flowers?"

Lottie waved her
wand and there was
a burst of magical
sparkles. A gorgeous
red lollipop in the
shape of a rose
appeared on the
picnic table. The
goblins howled with rage.

"One lollipop flower isn't enough for
Jack Frost's garden!" the smallest goblin
yelled. "You promised us lots and lots!"

"And you'll get lots more," Lottie
replied, "*when* you've cleared up the
litter like you promised."

Grumbling loudly, the goblins began
to pick up all the sweet-shop bags and
the lollipop wrappers and sticks. Lottie's
magic made Rachel and Kirsty human-

sized again, and they helped the goblins to throw the litter into the park bins.

Then Lottie waved her wand again. With a flash of glittering sparkles, four large green wheelbarrows appeared. Rachel and Kirsty saw that each wheelbarrow was crammed full with lollipops in the shape of flowers – daisies, roses, tulips, daffodils and giant lollipop sunflowers!

The goblins were thrilled. They dashed over to the wheelbarrows and examined the lollipop flowers with glee.

"These look good enough to eat!" the biggest goblin exclaimed.

"No!" groaned the other three goblins. "We feel sick!"

"You're the greediest goblin of all!" the smallest goblin told the big one. Squabbling loudly, each goblin grabbed a wheelbarrow and hurried away.

Lottie, Rachel and Kirsty grinned at each other.

"Girls, thank you for helping me get my magical lollipop charm back just before the big goblin took a bite!" Lottie laughed. "I couldn't have done it without you. And now I must return to the Fairyland Sweet Factory and give everyone the good news. At least now there will be lollipops for Treat Day!" And Lottie disappeared, leaving a faint mist of fairy magic behind her.

69

At the same moment, the girls suddenly noticed two pretty bouquets of flowers lying on the picnic table. When they looked a little closer, they realised the flowers were lollipops – pink roses, white tulips and yellow daisies.

Tucked inside each bouquet was a tiny note, written on glittery paper. The notes read: *Thank you for all your help, love from Lottie.*

"Aren't these lollipop flowers lovely?" Kirsty said happily, admiring her bouquet as she and Rachel headed back to Wetherbury high street.

"Yes, they're far too beautiful to eat, whatever the goblins say!" Rachel laughed.

As they neared the village sweet shop, the girls could see Tracy Twist outside, waving off some happy customers.

"Look, it's Mum and Aunt Harri!" Kirsty exclaimed. Hiding their fairy bouquets behind their backs, the girls ran to catch up with Mrs Tate and Aunt Harri. Rachel and Kirsty grinned at each other when they saw that both Mrs Tate and Aunt Harri were licking brightly coloured lollipops.

"Hello, girls," said Aunt Harri. "We've just popped in to see Tracy Twist, who's an old friend of mine, and she gave us these lollipops. They're delicious!"

"They certainly are," Kirsty's mum agreed.

"Maybe things are starting to get better at *Candy Land*," Aunt Harri murmured hopefully. "But I'm still worried. Although the lollipops are back to normal, we're still having a lot of other problems at the factory."

Kirsty glanced at Rachel. She knew exactly what her friend was thinking.

It was wonderful that they'd managed to find Lottie's lollipop charm. But Jack Frost was determined to build his candy castle, and it would be up to Rachel and Kirsty to stop him by finding the other six Sweet Fairies' magical objects!

Now it's time for Kirsty and
Rachel to help...

Esme the Ice Cream Fairy

Read on for a sneak peek...

"Bye, Aunt Harri," said Kirsty Tate, hugging her auntie. "It was really nice to see you again."

"Thanks for all the sweets," added Rachel Walker, Kirsty's best friend. She was staying with Kirsty over half-term.

Aunt Harri smiled at them. "My pleasure," she said. "I'm sorry they weren't as nice as normal though."

Kirsty's aunt had the best job in the world: she worked at *Candy Land*, the sweet factory just outside Wetherbury village. She'd come to have lunch with the Tates that day, bringing a big bag of *Candy Land* sweets for everyone with her. Unfortunately, the sweets had tasted terrible. Something had gone badly wrong!

The girls were disappointed but their dismay had quickly turned to excitement when their friend Honey the Sweet Fairy magically appeared in Kirsty's bedroom. She told them that strange things had been happening at her Fairyland sweet factory, and asked if they'd help her.

Kirsty and Rachel hadn't hesitated for a second. Of course they'd help – they loved going to Fairyland! And so, just moments later, they'd been swept up in another wonderful fairy adventure, this time with Honey and her team of Sweet Fairies. It had been the most perfect start to the half-term week, thought Rachel, smiling to herself.

The girls, Aunt Harri and Kirsty's mum were now standing outside Tracy Twist's sweet shop in Wetherbury High Street, where Aunt Harri was catching the bus back to work.

"I hope everything's working properly at *Candy Land* again," she said. "Still, at least the lollipops were nice."

"The lollipops were *delicious*," Kirsty replied, with a secret wink at Rachel.

Read Esme the Ice Cream Fairy to find out what adventures are in store for Kirsty and Rachel!

Meet the
Sweet Fairies

RAINBOW magic

Meet the fairies, play games
and get sneak peeks at
the latest books!

www.rainbowmagicbooks.co.uk

There's fairy fun for everyone on
our wonderful website.
You'll find great activities, competitions, stories and
fairy profiles, and also a special newsletter.

Competition!

The Sweet Fairies have created a special competition just for you!
In the back of each book in the Sweet Fairies series there will
be a question for you to answer. First you need to collect the
answer from the back of each book in the series.
Once you have all the answers, take the first letter from each one
and arrange them to spell a secret word!
When you have the answer, go online and enter!

We will put all the correct entries into a draw and select a winner
to receive a special Rainbow Magic Goodie Bag featuring lots of
treats for you and your fairy friends. You'll also star in a new
Rainbow Magic story!

Where do the Rainbow Magic Fairies live?

★ _ _ _ _ _ _ _ _ _

Enter online now at www.rainbowmagicbooks.co.uk

No purchase required. Only one entry per child.
One prize draw will take place on 31st July 2013 and 31st October 2013. Alternatively readers
can send the answer on a postcard to: Rainbow Magic Sweet Fairies Competition,
Orchard Books, 338 Euston Road, London, NW1 3BH. Australian readers can write to:
Rainbow Magic Sweet Fairies Competition, Hachette Children's Books, level 17/207 Kent St,
Sydney, NSW 2000. E-mail: childrens.books@hachette.com.au.
New Zealand readers should write to: Rainbow Magic Sweet Fairies Competition,
4 Whetu Place, Mairangi Bay, Auckland, NZ

Nicki the Holiday Camp Fairy

Rachel and Kirsty have been looking forward to camp, but everything is going wrong. Can they help Nicki fix things, before the whole summer is ruined?

www.rainbowmagicbooks.co.uk